THIS BOOK BELONGS TO:

____

Made in the USA
Monee, IL
08 June 2025

19062143R00069